Visitors From Mars

and Other Short Stories

Visitors From Mars
and Other Short Stories

Philip Sulumeti

EXCELLER BOOKS®
A GLOBAL PRESS

Visitors from Mars and Other Short Stories

Copyright © Philip Sulumeti, Kenya, 2024

Cover by Exceller Books using resources from Pixabay.com

ISBN: 978-81-19524-90-7

Published in India in 2024 by Exceller Books,
An imprint of GE Group

Address: G1, Dream Apartment, Degree College Road, Belgharia, Kolkata, 700056, India

www.excellerbooks.com

Dedication

This book is dedicated to my four children—Loraine, Purity, Ryan, and Russel—for the joy and fulfillment they bring me, which provided the peace of mind I needed to embark on writing.

Acknowledgement

I wish to acknowledge my wife, Marion, and my children—Loraine, Purity, Ryan, and Russel—for their unwavering support and patience during the long hours I spent writing this book.

Table of Contents

The Blurb

The eight short stories in this book are developed to capture the reader's imagination with captivating plots. It would be quite useful for senior school and college students who are seeking an entertaining pastime. It offers an opportunity to enhance their command of the English language as well as advance their writing skills.

In *Visitors from Mars*, a village in a remote kingdom finds itself at cross-roads when against all expectations, visitors arrive from the planet Mars, and they come to lay claim on their land! How should the humans react to the aliens?

In *The Evil Forest*, a lad is fed up with the age-old tales of a forest in the land feared as evil, to which nobody has ever set foot. Fired up by the desire to know the truth, he sets off on a solo mission into the forest. Even before he reaches its precincts, the spirits intervene, perhaps to save him from self-destruction.

A Glimpse of the City depicts the ironies that a young adult girl is faced with when she arrives in the capital city for the first time. She is uncertain of whether she will adapt to its strange ways. The stark difference between the two worlds is corroborated by what another young teenage girl finds out when she spends a holiday upcountry for the first time in *A Holiday in the Village.*

An Indelible Day presents an occasion that truly no student can ever forget. An otherwise festive and joyous day suddenly turns perilous. A young, naïve girl saves the day and takes all credit to become a living legend.

In *A Beast at Daybreak,* a woman wakes up to what promises to be a normal morning, only to encounter an enormous strange beast that she has never seen. She survives by a whisker. Villagers are subsequently treated to a series of dramatic events that is not only exciting, but also hair-raising.

In *A Prophetic Cloud,* 'a do or die' football match is hotly contested, pitting two rival teams with none willing to concede. What the losers did not know is that their fate had in fact been sealed beforehand.

A Twist of Fate is an intriguing tale of cattle rustling in rural Kenya. Two separate groups of rustlers unknowingly stage raids on each other's villages on the same night. This discovery creates a situation that is not only an awkward but also mind-boggling.

~ 11 ~

Visitors from Mars

A herder was grazing his cattle in an open field when a strange craft landed nearby. From the craft disembarked strange beings, half-humans, half machines. Their whole bodies were more compact and hardened, as though they carried no life in them. Their hands were shaped like wings. The aliens were more like aeroplanes than humans. They were a hybrid of sorts. The sight of the unusual beings unsettled him, leaving him uncertain of what to do. In any case, he was a long distance away from the nearest village, and nobody was in sight to come to his aid. In the short term therefore, he resigned himself to fate and waited to see what would happen.

The herder was astonished when the aliens spoke to him in his own mother tongue. "We are in Busoko kingdom, right?" their master inquired. "True," he answered with a shaky voice. "Who is the leader of the land"? "Chief Ubwasi" answered the herder. "Go fast and tell him that visitors from Mars desire to meet him", the master concluded with a solemn face. Right at that moment, the herder felt some invisible force push him away from the field, like the magnetic force of repulsion. At that point, he felt that he was extremely powerless in the face of the aliens, and his only option was to obey.

Visitors from Mars? For the next few seconds, the herder wished he were daydreaming. Visitors from another planet were unheard of anywhere in the world. What were they up to? Why had they chosen Busoko kingdom as their landing site? What did the future hold for the kingdom? He was lost in thought. The master spoke with a sense of urgency and the message had to be delivered fast, yet he wondered how the chief would even receive such weird news. Who would believe him?

Chief Ubwasi had just commenced taking his breakfast when the herder arrived at his compound. He was brought before him by the guards. The herder's face was telling. His heartbeat was loud and uneven. Something was terribly wrong. "What is it?" the chief asked pensively. "Strangers, they do not look like us," the herder responded. "Half humans, half birds, they have wings!" He added. The chief's mind went in circles. The herder was deemed to be of sound mind, and he did not mince with his words. There was no other interpretation of his message. In the chief's judgment, strange creatures had actually visited the land, and their mission was unknown.

It was at that time that Ubwasi remembered the counsel of his late father again: "Consult as much as possible and listen and listen again." Those were the words of wisdom that had shaped his decision-making over the years. They had never failed him. When therefore he decided to convene a meeting with the council of elders first thing, he knew it was the right thing to do. He cared little that the aliens urgently wished to see him. It was unlikely that aliens from Mars would come in peace. He had to find out the best way to defend his kingdom. In case he made a mistake and 'sold off' the community, he would be blamed solely. In a worst-case scenario, he could be forced to relinquish the crown. He would rather fail with the council than make a unilateral decision.

At the meeting, Ubwasi was presented with a host of ideas, ranging from outright surrender to total defiance. Out of wisdom, Ubwasi knew that the answer lay somewhere in between. At that point, he knew that he had to seek the perspective of elder Omwami. He was a decorated elder with remarkable wisdom. He usually talked last, yet his words would carry the day. Nobody lacks critics anyway, and Okuchi was one of them. He would go to a great length to belittle Omwami, explaining that the latter's perceived wisdom was just some skilful listening. By talking last, Omwami would ensure he obtained the average views of others first. Omwami's reputation was however, beyond reproach, and at this time, the chief needed him most. "Let's proceed and meet the aliens first," Omwami pronounced. His answer was against the expectation of the whole council, yet everybody knew that it was final. The elders rose up and proceeded straight to the field, their hearts burning with curiosity.

Back in the field, the aliens had lost patience. They had already started demarcating the land! Of course, they were claiming what was originally their own. Yet only they themselves understood this fact. Either the earthlings would take a very long time to accept this truth, or they would never. It was almost a foregone conclusion that the humans would put up a fight. Yet surrendering to them was no option. There was a population explosion on Mars, and Earth was the only other habitable planet. For that reason, the aliens had chosen to proceed hastily with what they had come to do, regardless of how the earthlings would respond. They had hived off a large chunk of land for themselves when the council arrived, surrounded by a crowd of villagers.

When the elders and villagers first set eyes on the aliens, they were thrust into a state of confusion. Just as the herder had reported, the aliens were neither humans nor machines. Their hands were modeled as wings. What was most astonishing was that they moved by walking as well as flying! While they spoke the same language as the earthlings, their physical appearance was materially different. It was clear the humans needed considerable time to understand the visitors. They particularly needed to appreciate their capabilities and strengths. The humans were especially perturbed by the fact that the aliens seemed to be at ease with themselves. They were dividing up the land as one would divide his own! This notwithstanding the fact that the humans were all along gazing at them in bewilderment. So resolute were they in this endeavor that one could only infer one thing- they were at a point of no return.

Chief Ubwasi had studied the aliens for some time when he decided to attempt a conversation. "Who are you, and what do you want?" he inquired. At this point, their master lifted his eyes up and looked at Ubwasi straight in the eyes, the other members proceeding with the demarcation fearlessly. "We come from the planet Mars. This is our ancestral land, and we have come to retake it"! Everybody was taken aback. Their ancestral land? How true could this be? All along, the earthlings had been at a loss as to how to deal with the aliens, now that the dilemma had just been magnified. Nobody could imagine that beings from another planet could have descended from Earth. Despite the slim chances however, it was deemed prudent that a benefit of the doubt be given to them, at least at that time.

In the absence of a logical explanation of what the aliens were claiming, Chief Ubwasi pressed the master further. "This is how it happened", the master proceeded. Just before the missionaries arrived here, there was a period of time when this land experienced many human disappearances. In those days, many men and women went missing without a trace. None of them ever returned. All the disappearances happened at night. Victims were picked up on their way or outside their houses by forces too powerful for them. They were taken away in crafts like that (pointing to the craft that had carried them to earth). Since the crafts were noiseless, it was impossible for other humans to detect the movements. The humans were carried away and introduced to the planet mars. While on mars, they intermarried and multiplied. However, due to the difference in atmospheric conditions between Earth and Mars, human bodies undergo mutation to develop hardened muscles and flesh. Their hands developed into wings. To the earthlings, this explanation was beyond their comprehension.

When asked to explain why they had decided to come back to earth, the master simply stated that the planet Mars could no longer sustain its huge population. It was difficult for anybody to take the aliens at their word. As news spread of the tales of the strangers, so did the quest for answers. It was now clear that confirming the aliens' assertions required delving into the history of the land.

There was an old man who lived at the edge of the river. He was the only nonagenarian left. Udoka lived a lonely, humble life. Save for the usual greetings, he talked less and rarely interacted with other people. All members of his immediate family had passed away. Luckily, he enjoyed good health and largely fended for himself. Two days after the encounter with the aliens, the whole council decided to pay a special visit to the old man. And the king leaving his lavish palace to visit the humble abode of a man as poor as Udoka depicted the magnitude of the problem.

After ensuring that the old man was at ease with his unexpected guests, the king posed the desperate question. "Have you ever heard of any mysterious disappearances in this land?" Udoka took a long gaze at the roof of his grass-thatched hut, clearly trying to replenish his memory. It took less than half a minute, yet it was the longest time the elders had ever waited for an answer. During that time, the house went completely mute, all eyes transfixed on the old man. Luckily, Udoka had maintained his gaze on the roof. Otherwise, he would have taken those sharp stares with a lot of suspicion. What he did not know was that he was the most important person in the kingdom at that time. "I remember something like that", Udoka murmured. This initial answer was received with mixed feelings. If what the aliens were alleging was true, it would compel the humans to share their land with them. On the other hand, the aliens would effectively be their blood relatives, averting a bitter confrontation.

Udoka had not personally witnessed the disappearances. However, his grandfather had once told him of how the latter's uncle and a couple of others had vanished from their villages, never to return. There was no reason to doubt the old man. The king had purposely failed to reveal to him the reason for that inquiry lest he become influenced by personal opinion. Udoka lived a secluded life at the riverside, and it was unlikely that he had gotten wind of the happenings in the kingdom at that time. Moreover, the aliens had no connection with anybody in the land. Even if they had, Udoka was the least expected to be their agent. Apparently, the aliens were telling the truth, and reality was just beginning to sink.

It was back to the drawing board. The aliens were sons of the land and perhaps, even deserved sympathy! Even if they were not, the kingdom was least prepared to take on super human beings from another planet. Needless to say, the future of the kingdom had been plunged into uncertainty-What would happen if the aliens intermarried with humans? What culture would they introduce in the land? They could invite more Martians to come to earth. The greatest fear, though, was that due to their perceived superiority, they could overcome humanity and perhaps colonize them or even enslave them!

There were nonetheless, a few enthusiasts in the community who sought a solution to this calamity. They were the types that refuse to be bogged down even by the worst-case scenarios. They opined that having come back to earth, the alien bodies were expected to mutate back to ordinary human beings. This could eliminate their perceived superiority and the attendant fears. The aliens could also introduce advanced technology, medicine, or weapons to the kingdom. At that point, however, the future of the kingdom was a grey area that could only be unravelled with the passage of time.

The Evil Forest

In the land of Bafoyo, there existed a forest whose origin and existence were shrouded in mystery. The forest itself was greatly feared, almost revered, especially by the elderly. The beliefs had been passed on from generation to generation, and even questioning their validity was considered taboo. Evil forces were believed to operate in the forest, and no one even wished to venture into its precincts. The irony however, is that nobody really cared to uncover the truth. Tales of the forest spanned ages and were deeply embedded in the fabric of the society. Habel grew up on these tales.

The forest itself was real. Set on a virgin land where no one dared set foot, it had large imposing trees that formed broad canopies. From afar, the forest portrayed alluring beauty. The trees were indigenous and could only have been planted by nature. One could only imagine the cool and undisturbed aura that subsisted beneath. Villagers could sight numerous fruits, both edible and inedible, dangling enticingly atop. Monkeys and other wild animals could be seen jumping delightedly from one tree to another. It was deemed nature's paradise, and to imagine that evil forces resided here defied the conscience of many. One thing was certain in Habel's mind. If the forest was truly occupied by evil, then those spirits were well endowed. They surely were enjoying life. Nobody knew the truth though; yet nobody as well, was prepared to know it first.

Questions about the forest lingered in Habel's mind. Strange voices were believed to be heard from the forest. Habel vividly remembered one night when he had woken up from sleep at around 2.00pm. He heard some loud voices clearly emanating from the direction of the forest! It was as if a large crowd was noisily cheering a football match. A number of villagers confessed hearing the same voices that night! It is incidences like these that confounded even the most ardent critics of the traditional tales.

Most elders believed that witches depended on the forest to empower their charms. Another tale had it that the forest had been a large grave yard for a community in the years gone by. That incessant cries of babies could be heard from the forest was particularly disturbing. The truth lied somewhere. Either villagers were rightfully frightened about the forest, or their phobia was just but undue fixation. The forest was an enigma waiting to be uncovered, something of a mystic.

Habel had heard enough since childhood. Now as a lad, he was overcome by a spirit of inquiry and a sense of duty to himself and society. The evil forest had to be conquered! Knowing very well that nobody would support him, he was to keep it a top secret, lest it leaks. His parents would particularly be taken aback. That would not be the mind of a son they had brought up over the years. A disturbing controversy would be created by such a revelation as well. Habel was never known to be strong-hearted. Villagers would relate such sudden garnering of courage to the cult of devil worship. For that reason, he risked being isolated and regarded as a 'marked man'.

The odds were stacked against him. If he encountered forces of destruction in the forest, he would have only himself to blame. He would become the laughingstock of even the small boys who were keen to obey their parents' instructions. Where would he hide his shame? Someone had to find out the truth and this truth was owed to the future generation as well. To him, it was better to find out the truth rather than live in perennial fear of the unknown. Rather than being lumped together with the age-old cowards, he would rather be the sacrificial lamb.

What villagers did not know was that Habel's inner courage was burning like a fire. He focused on the positive. Suppose the community's view of the forest was just but a myth. This would relieve the community from the fear that had tormented it for ages. The revelation would project him as a hero. For that reason, he would be welcome to 'dine with the elders'. What is more, he would become a favourite with the girls, a young man's craving. In the history books, he would perhaps be the greatest man who ever lived in the land of Bafoyo.

On the material day, Habel woke up at the normal time, not wishing to raise suspicion. He helped his parents with the usual morning chores, dressed up and left. Shortly after setting out, a wave of fear gripped his heart. What really inhabited this land? Anything could be expected: ghosts or strange beings. If the tales were true, then the forces of destruction were spirits. How could he fight the spirits in the flesh? He would be lucky to come out alive. And how would he be traced, for not even his closest friends knew of his mission? One thing that motivated him greatly was that every successful person has had a bout of discouragement. Honour therefore belongs to those who overcome their fears.

Having walked for some two kilometres, he felt thirsty, pulled out his water bottle and sipped some water. He had proceeded for a few hundred meters when he was hit by intense fatigue. He could now clearly see the forest outlay a distance away. If he walked for another five hundred meters, he would reach the forest edge. At this point, there were no homesteads, as the community had avoided the forest and its surroundings entirely. He was now literally a lone ranger, and his fears were magnified. Dog-tired, he sat for a rest under a large sycamore tree. He had barely settled into the cool shade when he fell asleep.

He found himself at the forest entrance. Two faceless creatures, half men, the other half indescribable, came to arrest him. They were clothed in animal skin with drooping feathered ears. Their sight was ghastly. They dragged him to their 'chief'. "Young man, why have you come to test the spirits of the land? You have chosen to discover the secrets of the forest, and so you shall," the chief rumbled in a hoarse voice. At this point, he felt an invisible hand hold him tightly. The grip was as though the hand was made of piercing needles, only that they did not prick his palm. He wished he could ask for forgiveness, but the chief's determination was unwavering. "You shall be introduced to the land," the chief pronounced.

He was taken to a large field with an army of men. The men had crocodile-looking faces. Each one of them held in his right hand a curved machete with metallic spikes. He heard a voice talk to him- "These are the watchers of the forest. They would never allow anyone to go beyond the designated boundary. As soon as they spotted you, they brought your spirit here. From that spot where you lie, you are highly monitored, lest you make access and gain knowledge of the forest. If you did, your spirit must be imprisoned here forever. Note that your spirit can not be detained without the body", the voice concluded.

What did that portend for him? Habel marvelled from within.

As if to prevent him from escaping, the hand held him even more tightly and led him to a dark gorge. 'This is the place where the spirits of your dead ancestors live", the voice remarked. At that moment, Habel could clearly hear a mix of loud voices, the ones akin to those he heard that night. The voices seemed as though spectators were cheering a football match! He was dumbfounded. The scene was macabre. An eerie silence filled the air. "It is these spirits that you have offended most," the voice added. "Before we proceed further, you must be initiated into the culture of this land," it declared.

The hand pulled him to the edge of a narrow river only a few meters away. It baffled him that despite its proximity, the river itself had been invisible to him before! Suddenly, a crowd of mermaids emerged from the water, each holding a razor-sharp object. Stone-faced, they appeared to have conspired to inflict pain, debilitating pain. It was a nerve-wracking moment. "The spirits wait to test your blood", again he heard a voice from above! "You must also be hardened for the demanding encounter on the other side," the voice added. "What is on the other side?" Habel asked with a shaky voice. "Young man, you have deliberately chosen to step on hot charcoal. Were you not prepared to burn your feet?" the voice answered.

Habel instantly felt the invisible hand push him into the river. He watched helplessly as the mermaids scrambled for his flesh, each wishing to make the first cut! He cried out in pain as he awoke, already running away from the forest! That in itself was a mystery. He had never expected that someone could wake up running. Had the spirits set him up in motion? For this reason, he had left behind his water bottle, never to return for it.

It was a timely reprieve. For it was an encounter one would wish only for his worst enemy. As he came to his senses tens of meters away, he meditated upon the dream. Clearly, it was an enlightenment as well as a warning. Surely, he could not have been cleverer than all the villagers. He thought to himself. The dream was so vivid. Its implication was obvious—the forest was more evil than he had imagined. He had stretched his courage too far and had barely escaped self-destruction. So he started running again, lest the spirits caught up with him.

As long as he lived, Habel would never divulge this experience to anybody, for that would make the villagers mock him for life. He vowed never to make any other attempt. His wish however, was that in his lifetime, there would arise a person courageous enough to take on the forest. If there would ever be such, that person would be endowed with extraordinary powers. This is because the forest itself was more powerful than ordinary men. For that reason, the mystery of the evil forest lives on to this day.

A Glimpse of the City

Anita had just finished high school. Aunt Jerusha lived in the city, and Anita often wondered how it felt to live in a large town. When Jerusha arrived in the village and promised to take her along on the return journey, it was a fulfilment of a yearning. She had lived in the village ever since she was born and had no idea what the horizons held. How she longed to explore the world. It was a timely and deserving escapade. As eagerness overcame her, she prayed to God that she would at least live long enough to see that day.

It was wintertime in Kenya. If what she had learned in school was true, then days were expected to be shorter than nights. In this particular season though, Anita realized that the opposite was probably true. The more she waited for the day to materialize, the more she became impatient and restless. In that short period of time, everything seemed to take longer than usual. One particular incident would remain embedded in her mind. She had placed a sufuria of water on a meko to prepare Ugali, the family's favourite meal. She had gone outside shortly to wash some utensils. Shortly after, she came back hurriedly, anxious that the water had overboiled. As she added handfuls of flour to the water, little did she realize that the water had barely started warming up. She had to pour out everything to start afresh!

As Anita went to bed on the eve of the journey, thoughts raced through her mind. She attempted to figure out what was going on in the city. True, she had read some stories about Nairobi but could not perfectly predict what it held. The significance of the journey itself could not be over-emphasized. It would not only afford her some bragging rights but also a sense of class. Many are boys and girls who had not even dreamed of living in the village in the first place. Nevertheless, the wait would now be over in a night, and what is more, the prize of waiting had already been paid. It was now time to stimulate all her five senses, for the city was waiting to be uncovered.

Ant Jerusha had deliberately planned for a night journey so that Anita could have a feel of the city early in the morning. On the appointed day, they boarded the bus at dusk. The bus itself was classic. Its external appearance was so magnificent, making it look spectacular. The seats were warm and relaxing, accustomed to long-distance travel. The interior roof and wall surfaces were smooth and polished to a white sheen. With such an attractive mode of transport, Anita wondered why some people still chose to travel by aeroplane. Perhaps they simply wanted to be different, or they were obsessed with status. So comfy was the carrier that she easily drowsed off to sweet dreams, leaving Aunt Jerusha conversing alone. It was as if she had slept only for a wink when she felt Jerusha tap her on the shoulder. It was at 5.00 in the morning. They had covered seven hours from Busia to Nairobi in what seemed to her a very short span of time.

As they were ushered into the waiting room, Anita wondered why they did not proceed straight to the estate. Of course, it was still dark and the city buses had not yet started plying the routes. However, Aunt Jerusha had to warn her that city robbers operated under the cover of darkness. Therefore, it was advisable to wait until the daylight. Moreover, Jerusha had planned to do some shopping for the supplies they needed for the week. Anita was eager to catch the first sight of town. Were the views awesome? She had persevered this dilemma for many years in the village. Now reality was just a daybreak away. She kept peeping through the windows and the door just in case she could make out something.

As darkness ushered in the first light, Jerusha stood up and Anita knew it was time to go. She was surprised to discover that in this city, dawn itself was ushered in with style-noisy touts calling at passengers at the top of their voices. Some were using loudspeakers to emit some ear-piercing sounds, yet they suffered no bother! To Anita, this was an alarming signal of how city dwellers took care of each other if they ever cared at all. It seemed like a ghost of individualism reigned in the city. The city would have to climb a mountain to exorcise it.

Anita looked all around her and what a sight! Many tall buildings of different sizes and shapes. Their designs were not only impressive but also stylish. It was the sheer cleanliness of the streets however that caught her imagination. They were immaculately clean. It was difficult to imagine that there could be poor people who lived anywhere in this city, for the skyline and the roads below signified opulence.

Businesses had started opening when the city became awash with men. A multitude of people filled every corner, so many such that Anita wondered whether the city had suddenly 'given birth'. With such a huge population in Nairobi alone, she wondered how the villages still had people left in them. It was as if everyone had migrated to town. "Where do all these people come from?" she asked. "From the estates and villages", Jerusha answered. Either life in the city was so sweet, or some overwhelming distress had overcome them in their homes, Anita thought to herself. Only time will tell.

Anita's attention was then drawn to the urgency with which people were walking on the streets. She noticed that everybody was walking very fast as if some invisible force was pushing them from within. Even age had ceased to be a factor in this city. Many were the instances when she saw elderly men walking faster than the youth as if riding on experience. Were they rushing for some free money somewhere, or could it be that they were going so far? Seconds later, she saw a man alight from a bus. The man rushed in front of them and proceeded quite fast, only to enter the next building! That is when it dawned on her that walking fast in this city was in fact, a tradition. People walked fast, even if they were going nowhere!

Ant Jerusha pointed to an entrance as they approached a sign post." This is the supermarket", she remarked. On entering, Anita was taken aback by the sheer size of the outlet. Rows and rows of items were arranged on the shelves and floor. Virtually everything could be found here. Anita's eyes could not move off the items as she moved from shelf to shelf, exploring with her eyes. Many were the things she had never seen in life. The attractive way in which the items were arranged confirmed what she had learnt at school. She had gone half way through the supermarket when she realized that she had lost contact with Jerusha. Little did she realize that Jerusha was agitatingly searching for her as well. The two bumped into each other a few minutes later. As Jerusha admonished her never to stray away from herself, Anita felt a sense of embarrassment. As they left the supermarket shortly after, she was careful never to lose sight of her again.

The duo had walked for a few minutes when they heard a shout "my bag"! A woman's handbag had been snatched. Anita had just turned to look when she saw the thief pass the bag over to her accomplice, a lady in skinny jeans. Again, the sense of indifference from the crowd disturbed her mind. Were these people fearful of the thieves, or were they simply self-centred? Did they not have a sense of community? Anita was desperate for answers. The fact that even Aunt Jerusha did not give it any attention was more alarming. The woman attempted to chase the thieves, but the bag was changing hands quite fast. She gave up in tears. A lesson was instantly planted in her innocent mind that in this city, every man was for himself, and only God was for everybody else.

As they moved along the streets, Anita noticed that the city seemed to lack any sense of order. Large rows of people were moving in different directions, yet with no regard for each other. Those moving in opposing directions constantly rammed into each other head-on, yet nobody complained. Nobody acknowledged one another. It was as if everybody was a stranger in the city, much like herself. An ominous sense of loneliness was engraved in her mind. She knew she was to brace herself for a life of solitude in the estate. She now understood why even Aunt Jerusha was behaving the way she did. This city was capable of transforming even the most sociable people into something else. Anita wondered whether citygoers went to church. If ever they did, then they were likely a bunch of hypocrites waiting for judgment.

Aunt Jerusha pointed to bus number 32 just as it was slowing down to stop. As she stepped on the stairway, Anita was glad to have had a glimpse of the city. It was a relief just on time. In her mind, the city was 'stranger than fiction'. She needed time to comprehend and accept its mannerisms. Staying longer in the city would only unsettle her further. It did not help matters that Aunt Jerusha seemed at ease with everything. If only she had been explaining to her the reason the city behaved the way it did. The driver pressed his foot against the accelerator. It pleased Anita that she was effectively escaping from the city and its ironies, at least for that day.

An Indelible Day

The day Naomi had been waiting for was finally here. The school prize-giving day was an occasion that occurred only once a year, and everybody knew it would be a colourful event. All and sundry had been full of anticipation. They had been waiting for the day with zeal and zest. To add the icing on the cake, the day would provide a break from the usual monotonous routine.

She got out of her cosy bed, leaving the bed sheets swirling behind her. At dawn, the sun bounced out of its cocoon, ushering in daytime and making the grass shimmer like broken pieces of glass. She proceeded to the bathroom and had a warm shower. It left her feeling as cool as a cucumber. The warm shower especially thrilled her. She often shuddered at the thought of students having a cold shower in boarding schools. For that reason, she had managed to convince her parents to maintain her in a day secondary school, notwithstanding the strong resistance from her friends.

Afterwards, Naomi walked back to her room. She wore her best-fitting and newest uniforms. A bow hanging down her neck gave her an exquisite look. There would be guests at school, and the school principal had instructed the girls to make their best attempt at appearing gorgeous. As she descended down the spiral staircase, the sweet aroma of spiced tea called out to her. Her mother would normally stop at nothing to ensure she had a satisfying breakfast. As fast as a deer she went, taking two steps at a time. She eagerly devoured her luscious meal.

As Naomi started off to school, she could not help but imagine what the day would look like. The school administration had invited the area member of parliament—what a luminary to grace the occasion! As would be expected, the students had been required to decorate every nook and cranny. This they did with enthusiasm until the ambience looked eye-catching. The guest of honour was an important person in the society, and it was necessary to create an atmosphere befitting her status. Moreover, the traditional African belief was that improvements would be made in the home whenever a visitor was coming. Naomi however wondered whether the administration had not overdone it, for the beauty of the school on that day was exceedingly appealing. Everything looked elegant.

After attending to the finer details, the principal was convinced that preparations had reached fever pitch when he called the school to order. All the students were required to assemble at the school gate. They were then instructed to line up on both sides of the road leading from the gate, ready to welcome the guest of honour.

The brand new red hummer that halted at the gate looked glorious. The lady spent the first few minutes acquainting herself with her new environment. Finally, she came out. Woh! Naomi had never imagined such magnitude of splendour in a woman. She looked like a million dollars. Her dress was a designer piece, with a lilac and ivory colour scheme that matched impeccably with her silver earrings. Her shoes were high-heeled, making her walk with an elevated ego. As she walked along, the shoes cried out 'quee, quee, quee', announcing her riches. In her hand she held a brief case larger than life.

Affluence is not the only thing that defines this woman, however. Some people seem to have been endowed with just everything that life requires. She was a tall, medium-built lady of a dark complexion, the perfect definition of African beauty. Her long, curly hair flowed over her shoulders, enhancing her radiant appearance. The colossus looked glamorous. So resplendent the lady was that the guests and pupils watched her every step from the gate to the meeting hall. Needless to say, the lady was as courageous as she was confident, for any shy person would simply falter under such heightened attention.

The boisterous crowd clapped exuberantly as the guests took their seats. The master of ceremonies, who was 'dressed to kill', took over. "Welcome all to this auspicious occasion", he started off. "It occurs once in a blue moon", he added.

It was time for the school choir to demonstrate their prowess again. A round of applause was given as they, Naomi included, went to the podium. They had prepared a short song for the day. It was then that Naomi scanned the sea of humanity in attendance. Yes, the principal had gotten it right. Inviting the area Member of Parliament had worked just as it had been anticipated. She was a crowd-puller. Villagers had not just come to attend the event but rather also ask for handouts from the 'Mheshimiwa'. The lady had a large, shiny handbag with her, which could only act to cool the villagers' anxiety. Everybody knew what was inside.

No sooner had the choir been okayed by the master of ceremonies than Naomi saw two strange men enter the hall. They proceeded straight to take the back seats. Naomi smelt something fishy in the stranger's intentions. She had learnt to trust her instincts over the years. However, she did not wish to give it much thought at that time, for with all those eyes gazing at them on stage, she couldn't. Therefore, she let bygones be bygones and focused on what they had to do at that moment. They sang lyrically on stage. As if to motivate them, guests swung their heads rhythmically from side to side. It was an electrifying performance that left the audience mesmerized.

As the choir left the podium, Naomi could feel a sense of relief, for they had yearned to impress their guests and they had, in fact, delighted them. No doubt the performance had set the mood for the day. At that point, the day seemed full of promise and excitement. Flamboyant faces could be observed in every corner as the guests appeared eager for the next activity.

Naomi had warmed her seat only for a few seconds when she remembered the two strange men at the back of the hall. Her anxiety returned. Nevertheless, not all nightmares come true in real life. With this conviction, she hoped for the best and once again, tried to concentrate on the events of the day.

All protocol had been observed when the master of ceremonies invited the Member of Parliament to the podium. No sooner had she stood up than some horrifying gunshots rent the air! Everybody shuddered in horror. It was an unexpected turn of events at the point when the celebration had reached a climax. The two men were heading for the briefcase. "Hand it over", they ordered in horsy voices. They were humongous and furious. That is when reality hit the Member of Parliament like a thunderbolt. Naomi felt her heart beat spasmodically inside her chest. A chill ran down her spine with every passing second. Her mind spun. The men were on top of their game as everybody scampered for safety. They portrayed a picture of seasoned robbers who could only be stopped by a miracle!

If anything could stop these men, then it had to come as a surprise, Naomi knew, for they seemed to anticipate all conventional sources of defence from their victims. Maybe she was born for this day, but she struggled to convince herself. The robbers would hardly expect a vicious attack from a girl as young and naive as Naomi. Against this backdrop, she moved closer to the centre of the action. She quietly sneaked behind the man with the pistol, for the men were too engaged to notice.

There was a rope hanging down from the roof, and Naomi saw it as God-sent. She held the rope tightly, lifted her legs up and used them to hit the gunman hard on his back. The man's spinal cord must have suffered a major fracture, leaving it with no strength. He fell down with a thud! The accomplice surrendered in fear. Police were called and arrived swiftly. However, in the spirit of mob justice, the two men had been manhandled. Phew! It was a sigh of relief.

As soon as the Member of Parliament had regained her composure, the girl who had probably saved her life was brought before her. She was lost for words. The hearty embrace she gave the girl was captured in photographs in major newspapers the following day. It was a crowning moment for Naomi. The crowd could not believe that a young teenage girl had overcome two beastly robbers where male body guards had cowered in submission. The story caught the imagination of the nation a few days later. At that point, even male chauvinists seemed to resign to the emerging dictum that 'what a man can do, a woman can do better'.

The ceremony continued, but everybody knew that there were now two important people in the hall. She was still basking in her newfound glory when the guest of honour was given a list of students who were to be recognized for academic excellence. As she rose up to receive her prize, a feeling of euphoria engulfed her. She was on 'cloud nine'. Her parents, who were in attendance, were full of the joys of spring. What a daughter they had brought up!

Naomi had single-handedly prevented a cheerful occasion from turning into 'doomsday'. The events of that day had made her a celebrity in the land, a living legend. As she stepped out of the school gate that evening, she was certain that she would never forget that day in her diary, unless of course, pigs fly!

A Beast at Daybreak

Nakhulo had just woken up from a long night's sleep. Being an early riser, she had gotten used to the dawn darkness over time. However, nothing had prepared her for what was waiting outside her compound at such an hour. This was going to be a morning like no other, even though nothing had appeared foreboding.

She calmly opened her wooden door and gently stepped outside. She first looked to the left, which appeared blank, just as she had expected. Then she gazed at the right, and hell broke loose! She wished it was a horror movie. A huge creature with short horns and a weird-shaped face stood right there, staring at her keenly. It appeared heavily built, stout and ready to charge at the slightest provocation. The creature seemed to have been anticipating and prepared for a commotion with the woman! The outlook was grim.

Rather than gather the energy to run, Nakhulo was thrust into a state of indecision. If she ran away, the act could incite the beast to pursue her. Ever since she was a child, her parents had admonished her never to run away from a barking dog. The act would certainly incite the dog to a hot pursuit. She was not certain that this beast would act differently. If she gathered courage and stood transfixed to the ground, the beast could perceive her as easy prey! Whatever the choice, her life hung on a thin thread. She wished she could shout for help. However, she realized that the fright in her had reduced her voice to a whisper. She stood there motionless, hoping for a miracle. Her prayer was answered.

The beast seemed to have realized that the woman posed no danger and simply turned away.

Marauding, it ran downwards, destroying maize and cassava crops on its path. It was at this point that Nakhulo regained strength and shouted for help. A number of villagers responded and soon formed a crowd. They gave the animal a chase. A few minutes later, the beast reached Mr. Ingotse's compound. He had just stepped outside to release his chickens when he saw the beast running straight towards him. As he hid behind the chicken house, he had expected it to proceed along the path running between the two houses. He was wrong. Desperate for a place to hide, it dashed into his sitting room!

Curious villagers surrounded the house, trying to figure out how to 'smoke' it out. Other than wishing to know the true identity of the beast, the overriding motivation was to drive away danger from their midst. There was one insane man in the crowd who started beating a metallic drum while making a lot of noise. The noise seemed to irk the animal even more, making it both agitated and infuriated. Suddenly, it charged out of the house menacingly. Everybody was caught unawares as men and women fell on top of each other like piles of wood! Before they could wake up to respond, the animal had gained ground and was running towards the river. Another chase commenced, but villagers had now learnt from experience.

A group of men ran sideways and attempted to intercept the animal from their wing, as the second group ran from the other side. Soon afterwards, the animal felt cornered and decided to put up a fight. It stopped, faced the crowd head-on and gave out a loud cry. It was the type of cry that every animal gives out when it realizes that its chances are slim, yet it has to give the last kick. Everyone stopped in panic, for the sound of its screaming depicted anger and revenge. Villagers could now feel each other's heartbeat as nobody knew whether the animal could decide to charge again and in which direction. The spectacle however, also provided an opportunity for villagers to separate 'boys from men' At that point in time, only men of valour stood to be counted. Who would steal the show?

Darkness had started waning when villagers decided to take a hard look at the animal. Oh! it was a hippo! Hippos live in water and none had ever ventured into the village. What could possibly have driven it from its safe abode? Certainly, it must have strayed out of Lake Victoria through the nearby river Sio. The drought had persisted, forcing many animals to venture into unfamiliar surroundings in search of food.

Omogo lifted his eyes up and surveyed the crowd. He realized that, apart from him, there was a noticeable lack of bravery in the crowd. The only other person who could have complimented his courage was Omondo. The latter however, had overdrunk *changaa*, the local brew from Mama Pima. The lady was famed for selling imported liquor from neighbouring Ubanga, christened in the local language as 'moja kwisha'. The name meant the liquor could knock someone out with just the first glass. If only Omondo was around, the work would be considered half-done. Somebody had to act fast, however. It was either the animal gets killed, or it kills somebody; there is no middle ground. Omogo enjoyed a psychological advantage, though. Not long before then, he had surprised villagers when he engaged an armed robber, snatching a gun from him with bare hands! He knew the whole village counted on him, and his reputation was at stake.

Omogo moved quietly to the back of the animal. He courageously drew his machete and struck its upper leg. It groaned in pain but charged at the crowd aimlessly. Everyone understood that the animal, in its agony, was ready to take someone down with it. They ran away like seasoned athletes. It was at this point that Epelu, the chief's grandson, appeared from nowhere. He threw his spear that pierced through the animal's neck. It fell on its ribs.

No sooner had the animal breathed its last than the scramble for its meat began! It was interesting to see how the most cowardly persons became the first to lay claim to the meat. Such were the ones that could not even stand the hippo's cry of agony. It was every man for himself as women helplessly watched as men threatened to slice each other's hands. If a woman's husband did not pursue the animal, she would have nothing to take to her children. Nevertheless, the day itself provided some exceptionally entertaining drama. No villager had ever set eyes on such a huge and strange creature in a live environment, and it would probably never happen. Despite the menacing episodes of the beast charging severally, many were glad that they had witnessed the events of that day, the day that had made them tourists in their own village.

That morning, smoke could be seen rising from homesteads as villagers prepared to commence roasting in earnest. The selfish ones had collected free meat for the whole week. Hence, as they retired to their beds later in the evening, many wished against hope that, out of the blue, another hippo would stray into the village.

It was a morning filled with contradiction. If only the villagers had known how it had started at dawn, that heart-rending sight Nakhulo endured for several seconds. At that moment, her life came to a halt. Instead of celebrating with the villagers, she wished the day away, seeking solace wherever she could find it. She was lucky to be alive. The villagers would feast on the meat, many for a couple of days. That was likely the time the beast would have needed to digest her flesh! For that reason, she had vowed never to feast on a beast that would have devoured her instead.

A Prophetic Cloud

Milema woke up with the birds, just in time to hear their melodious songs. The air was filled with soothing music from nature. As he got carried away by the rhythmic sounds, he started humming. How he wished to pause for some time to savour the heart-warming moment. Yet the excitement of the day was too much to tame. He hurriedly proceeded to check on his friend Achoka, whose dormitory was only a few meters away. He walked straight to his bed. "Wake up, it is sports day," he exclaimed. The two had engaged in a lengthy discussion the previous evening, comparing their football team with other schools. They concluded that it would be a herculean task for any team to beat them in a fair match. The much-awaited tournament was finally here. Would they vindicate themselves?

Not all agreed with the two comrades, though. Nderema School had posted mixed results in the previous matches. Two years ago, they were beaten 2–0 by the then-emerging Simenya School. The memory of this loss was still fresh in everybody's mind. In the previous event, however, Nderema bounced back to form. They had beaten Sirikwa School in the intra-county finals. For that, they won away the coveted title of county champions. A somersault pass that Edwiny did to move the ball to Bansey, who in turn got the goalkeeper totally off guard, was still celebrated until then.

The bell rang for breakfast and all the students assembled in the dining hall. Heated arguments could be heard from various tables as each person attempted to predict the results between teams. On that morning, the dining hall was like a marketplace, with inaudible loud noises filling the air. Tenth-grade students were particularly lucky as bully Stano had been sent home for fees. He would bully his way even with arguments, not willing to accept contrary views. Many were the times when simple arguments degenerated into fistfights, courtesy of his intolerance. Harsh name-calling was unavoidable, resulting in additional work for the hawkish prefects. Luckily, the bell rang just in time, and everyone was required to proceed to the assembly. In the excitement of the arguments, many had forgotten to take their tea, forcing them to take whole cups in single sips!

Housekeeping rules were read to students by the deputy head teacher, Mr. Makhalwa. Students were required to be welcoming and courteous to visitors. The reputation of the school was at stake, as any misconduct would be noticed by other schools. Mr. Makhalwa was known to be a disciplinarian, and students took his word as law. They feared him like thunder, and who else was best placed to pass on such a solemn message? The head teacher reminded the students of the school motto: ' Rise above and shine', a rallying call to the team to aspire for victory even in the face of a strong opponent. No sooner had the visitors' buses started arriving than the students were released to go to the field. Each team was allocated a place for preparation and warm-up.

Milema knew very well that, being the hosts, they would be the first to play against their opponents. Who would it be? The referee approached the midfield, and everybody's eyes were transfixed to the pitch. Jointly with the coaches, they engaged in a draw as the results were eagerly awaited. It was Msoma School! Msoma was a seasoned team with a history of 'poaching' the best players from other schools to perfect performance. If ever there was a time when luck seemed evasive for Nderema, this was it.

Football match results, however, were deemed predictable only by angels. Skills seemed not to be the only forces governing performance. Some mysterious forces operating from places unknown appeared to influence results. History was awash with instances when less celebrated teams won against football *gurus*, and the most experienced players failed to convert penalties into goals. Anxiety was apparent on Milema's face as Msoma's school team arrived at the midfield. The elation on the opponent's face did little to calm his fears. It was a date with destiny.

Milema lifted his eyes to the sky, as if asking for the intervention of a higher power. A small dark cloud hung in the sky right above the pitch. The referee blew his whistle, and Msoma School started off. Their players engaged in some high-speed manoeuvres coupled with several precision passes. Nderema players were reduced to chasing the ball as their opponents made exploits. They were however, playing on home ground, and there was no reason to lose optimism. With this spirit, Ambani, Nderema's midfielder, made remarkable tackles, repeatedly winning possession of the ball. It was not until the thirty-sixth minute however, that expectations peaked. At that moment, Msoma's Amoke brought down Nderema's Sime in the forbidden area. It was a penalty!

Nderema's captain was the undisputed choice for the duty. He adjusted the ball at its spot, moved back fervently and held his hands akimbo. He then gave the goalkeeper a sober look. It was the type of gaze that could drain away confidence from any goalkeeper who relied on looks rather than faith. He moved forward steadily and hit the ball at an angle. Unfortunately for him, the ball hit the goalpost and rebounded straight into the hands of the goalkeeper! The latter hurriedly threw the ball to his players, who were keen to launch a counterattack. With that inspiration, Kenga moved with supersonic speed to the midfield and then gave a long pass to Kabuya at the flank. Kabuya gave a pass to Sifa in the penalty area. Then it happened!

Nderema's Matoke had rushed in to intercept, closing in on Sifa. Some scoring opportunities in a football match last only for split seconds, and Sifa was aware of that fact. Oblivious of Sifa's options, Matoke spread his legs too wide. Obstructed, the goalkeeper was caught off guard as the ball went through his legs. For them, it was a 'double tragedy'. A sombre mood engulfed Nderema School as the first half ended a few minutes later.

The second half began, and Nderema School seemed to have taken their coach's instructions to heart. Of course they knew they were racing against time. They carried the hopes of their school. A loss in the tournament would plunge the entire school into melancholy. They started off the match with a high speed, coupled with smart passes. Granted, this resulted in an enviable ball possession. However, their opponents were not prepared to lose the 'golden egg' already in their basket. Despite the slim chances, Nderema School made spirited efforts to redeem their ego. They put up a final display of skill and tact that was nothing short of exemplary.

Attacks were made against counterattacks, yet neither side scored a goal. On the other hand, time seemed to have acquired wings. The referee blew his final whistle, and it was absolutely over! At that point in time, many in Nderema School thought it was a dream. As they came to terms with reality a few minutes later, some wished the ground would open up and swallow them alive! Only a few recognized that they had at least lived to fight another day. They had been bitten on home ground. With their reputation stained, they knew they would have to live with that humiliation for the foreseeable future.

Milema looked up to the sky, this time seeking consolation. He remembered the dark cloud that had hung above the pitch. It was at that time that it dawned on him that the cloud was in fact, a premonition.

A Twist of Fate

On that evening, Musonye went to bed quite late, as if he was watching over something. There was a sense of disillusionment in his mind, the source of which he could not explain. He wished he could drift off to sleep earlier. However, he realized that his eyes were kept wide open as if suffering from insomnia. What could possibly have gone wrong? Or was something about to go wrong? As he struggled to gain sleep in the middle of the night, he hoped against hope that all would end well.

Having slept barely for two hours, Musonye woke up. He felt an extreme state of calmness that prevailed at that hour of the night. It was quiet and still, a promise of peace and rest, so he thought to himself. What a tranquil night it was. That his preliminary fears stood to be confirmed in that atmosphere of restfulness was the least of his expectations. Just as he turned his head to face the wall, he heard some commotion in the cowshed. The movement and mooing of the cows were peculiar. It pointed to one thing: a stranger in the byre.

Musonye got out of bed. He cast his spying eyes through the curtains. Two men were standing at the entrance to the cowshed. A third man was right inside, untying the cows! He had to act fast. His family had painstakingly nurtured the cows over the years. He could not allow thieves to make away with them. With an iron bar in his hand, he proceeded with stealth. He envisaged that he would ambush the thieves and then clobber them on their heads in quick succession.

It almost worked. However, just as he approached the cowshed, he entangled himself against a log of wood. He stumbled and fell. The sound of the fall alerted the thieves. One of them pointed a strong light straight into his eyes. Ooh no! It was a defensive torch. His vision blurred completely. His limbs suddenly became wobbly, and his whole body was trembling. The man pinned him tightly to the ground, pressing a foot on his back. With his face downwards, he was literally forced to kiss the ground. "You must learn to curb your bravery, you fool", the man whispered, wary of waking up other family members. "You utter a word, and this machete will slice your neck," he warned sternly. Musonye could only wish for reprieve.

He regained consciousness and noticed that the cowshed was empty with nobody in sight. Was it all lost? Never! Like a wounded lion keen to retaliate, he woke up majestically. The thieves had to be intercepted. If anything, they were armed with simple weapons like machetes, for he had spotted no gun. For that reason, he perceived them as some down-to-earth cattle rustlers. On that night, the moon was shining on a clear blue sky. This meant that it was easier to trace the raiders' path. Nevertheless, he had to strategize in a blink of an eye. First things first, he shouted for help.

Luckily, his father had just woken up. The shouts of his son outside depicted a distress call. In confusion, he rushed outside, not certain of what to expect. In a state of soul searching, he glanced through the cow shed, only to notice its emptiness! He had lost the family's only source of value. He fainted and fell. Luckily again, Musonye's mother had just woken up, courtesy of the noise from the two men outside. Mother had just arrived to attend to her husband when Musonye dashed after the raiders. It was at that point that the wails of her agitated mother caught the attention of the village. Men streamed out of their houses almost in unison. They were certain of one thing- the village had suffered another raid.

Cattle raids had become rampant not just in Limara but in the entire division. Villagers had vowed to punish the raiders severely if they ever caught up with them. What the thieves did not know was that the entire village had been waiting for them. Villagers were not only expressing solidarity with the Musonyes, but were also keen to pre-empt another raid. Never once had the entire village responded to distress like a calling!

Inspired by footmarks, Musonye led the men with clinical precision. The game plan was to run ahead of the raiders and then confront them from the front. Speed was of the essence, and the villagers knew that time, like seasons, waits for no one. Swiftness would afford a double advantage as the raiders would inevitably be slowed down by the pace of the cows. The chase itself was full of incidents. There were falls, stumbles and bruises. The worst moment was when Adika, who had never done any night duties, got lost in the forest. For several minutes, the party had to abandon the mission in an attempt to trace him. Luckily, Amakobe had brought his hunting dog along. The dog spotted him just before he could reach the edge of a cliff. It would have been a tragic ending for him- a mess of flesh soaked in blood!

At the first strike of dawn, Musonye heard for the first time, some faint sounds of what seemed like the mowing of cows. Inspired, villagers garnered remnants of strength as they pushed their bodies to the limit. It was a moment worth celebrating, all-be it inwardly. The raiders were about to be cornered, even though they may not have been aware of this fact. Plans to punish the 'devils' were hatched in the minds of the villagers. Some wanted outright execution, some lynching mob justice style. Bizarre suggestions could not escape the imaginations of some- a few people contended that the raiders should be taken back to Limara and made a permanent display in the village square, as though in a museum. At that instant, it was reasonable to conclude that the raiders were staring at a bleak time ahead.

There was an open valley a few hundred meters ahead. Any experienced raider would avoid driving cattle through this stretch, especially if he knew he was being pursued. The bare plain would place anything and anybody into perfect vicinity. The pressure from the pursuers however was growing closer by the minute. The raiders were running out of options and their only hope at that time was hinged on luck.

Just as Musonye's eyes peered through the valley for the first time, he saw the cows emerge from the forest, the same forest that was concealing the villagers behind. These were his family's cattle being driven away! One thing cast doubt on the recovery effort nonetheless- nobody knew with certainty the raiders' exact number. It was thus impossible to know whether they had been outmanned. This apprehension was however, deemed insignificant as Musonye's side had an army of men lurking in the bush.

Something strange was about to happen that would catch everyone off guard. Just as the villagers were closing in on the raiders, another heard of cattle emerged from the opposite forest! A few minutes later, five men chasing after the cattle surfaced from behind. They had raided Eskova village in Ndola Sub County. Armed with machetes and waist swords, they appeared ready to vanquish anybody who would stand in their way. As the spectacle unfolded across the field, Musonye tried to figure out how it would impact the course of the mission.

Even before Musonye and his men could accost their culprits, a large group of pursuers from Eskova village emerged from the forest. They were armed with all sorts of crude weapons, and vengeance was written all over their faces. Their determination was unassailable. It was a do-or-die affair. As the two herds of cattle approached each other, it was inevitable that raiders and pursuers would meet at the centre. Everybody prepared for a vicious fight. Gosh! There was going to be bloodshed in the valley. Musonye shuddered at this prospect, yet as the primary victim, he had to manifest the greatest courage. He attempted a prayer. He murmured a few words, but his lips went dumb, for the enormity of the situation was greater than his faith.

The raiders and the cattle were now only a few meters ahead. Musonye adjusted the iron bar on his right hand to have a tight grip. If he succeeded in hitting a raider on the head, he wouldn't even make the last shout of agony. He lifted the iron bar high over his shoulders. Just before he could bring it down to 'shade blood', his eyes met with those of Ambisi, a fellow villager from Limara! He was on the opposite side, one of the rustlers having raided Eskova. At the same time, there was simultaneously name-calling between pursuers and raiders from opposite sides!

It was a farfetched coincidence. Two sets of pursuers and raiders acting independently met at one spot! For that reason, an interesting discovery was awaiting. The rustlers had raided directly from each other's villages! This meant that each group of rustlers was well known to pursuers from the other side. It was an unnerving moment. In the confusion that followed, nobody was certain of whether to exchange pleasantries or to attack. In any case, everybody was either busy in conversation with the other side or was caught up in deafening, awkward silence. The cattle roamed freely around the field, neglected without a shepherd. They were tasting freedom for the first time.

It was a moment of reckoning for pursuers. If each group insisted on attacking its villains, then their kin would certainly fall victim to pursuers from the other side. The villains would almost certainly receive support from their kin of pursuers from the opposite side as well.

What an unexpected ending. Pursuers had prepared and were armed for retribution. The raiders had literally surrendered to death, more so because they had been grossly outnumbered. Their assailants would have been pleased to 'skin them alive'. At best, they would be 'bitten to pulp'. How could such a night have ended in peace? Anything that would save a man on such a day could only be attributed to the super natural.

It was a bittersweet truth. The chase had ended without bloodshed, yet each community realized it had harboured a bunch of heartless rustlers. This truth was heartbreaking to the innocent majority. Musonye was nevertheless relieved, for the recovery itself was a soothing ending to an otherwise traumatizing night.

A Holiday in the Village

When Melisa's father arrived home from work that Friday, nothing seemed out of the ordinary. He would normally remove his shoes at the door and then proceed straight to the bedroom for a change. Without resting, he would then stroll to the dining room for his evening tea, usually without uttering a word. Woe unto the house girl if the tea was not ready! On this particular evening, Dad pulled a seat at the dining table. He then looked at her straight in the eyes. "We are all going up-country tomorrow"! He uttered with a beaming face.

Born and brought up in the city of Kisumu, Melisa was essentially a town girl. Many times, she would beg her father to take her along to the village, but her incessant pleas often fell on deaf ears; how she wished to see her grandmother and spend time with her. She had heard from her classmates how pampering grandmothers can be. A friend had once told her how her grandma had scolded her mother for forcing her to wash her own clothes! If that was true, then grandmothers were actually sent from heaven. Her only wish was that her own was no different.

Several questions were seeking answers in her mind. She wanted to know how people lived in the village. What kinds of meals were eaten there? How did children in the village go to school, and what did those schools look like? Was there adequate security in the village, and was it even an issue at all? What was it like working on the farm? Her mind was rife with inquisition. This time around however, there was an opportunity to separate 'chaff from the grain'. It was like going on a tour in a foreign land oblivious to its way of life. No doubt the holiday promised to be as eventful as a wedding ceremony. For this reason, she would have a myriad of stories to tell her classmates when schools re-opened.

When Melisa and her family took off from the city in the family car, she had painted a picture in her mind of how the homestead would look like. She was wrong. On arrival, her eyes glanced through a ring of grass thatched houses of different sizes. That is when it dawned on her that she would probably sleep in a grass thatched hut that night! The beauty of the green lush trees that created superb serenity was nonetheless a source of solace.

To her surprise, grandfather had invited a host of relatives and villagers to welcome their entourage. They had all honoured the invitation. Melisa wondered how some people would be concerned about others, yet they did not mean anything in their day-to-day lives. Were they simply bored with nothing else to do? They soon settled down after a brief introduction. That is when Melisa started to monitor events keenly. She was not even sure of what behaviour to manifest. She was mindful not to exhibit mannerisms that would be frowned upon by her grandparents, for the culture here seemed different.

First, there was a cow shade, and Melisa noticed that her grandmother had just started milking a lactating cow. Throughout her life, she consumed only packed milk. This was an opportunity to witness for the first time how milk is extracted from the cow's teat. It was amazing. However, she also observed that the cowshed was littered with some fresh-smelling cow dung. Her grandmother, on the other hand, seemed unbothered. Was she indifferent to the filth? There arose a contest in her mind as to whether or not to ask her grandmother that question, but her courage failed her.

Melisa had been overcome with curiosity when she looked to the left. She saw a small, rounded structure with a grass-thatched roof. She pointed to it, and her grandmother mentioned to her that it was a grain store. It was indeed a traditional granary. Melisa noticed that it had an entrance, yet it did not have a door to close. Are there no thieves here? She asked, to which her grandmother replied emphatically, "No"! It was difficult for her to imagine that thieves could fail to steal easily available food that was not secured. Back in the city, 'tight security' was a phrase on everybody's lips. Perhaps the village had enough food for everybody, she mused.

As soon as supper was ready, the family assembled at the dinner table. All the relatives and invited friends joined in too. Apart from what she had learnt at school, it was the first time Melisa had witnessed an extended family setting. She noticed that villagers and other relatives even ate from the same plate! What a sense of friendship it was, or was it premitivity? Possibly, it was a blend of the two. The meal itself was a discovery. It had been cooked in a traditional cooking pot, giving it an exotic taste. Raw milk had been added to grandma's favourite vegetables- the 'chimbokas'. The local Murenda vegetables had been spiced with ash obtained from burnt sorghum-the 'Muhereha'. She was hungry, yet she was not sure how these meals would taste. Luckily, there was a burning desire that was pushing her to try out everything new. What experiences would she carry back to the city anyway?

On that night, Melisa retired to bed, of course, in a grass-thatched hut. Her mind was full of denial as to how people were able to catch sleep in such a house. Dry grass is most flammable and could easily catch fire. What if a malicious person ignited the grass? A child acting innocently could also ignite the grass! She wished she could stay awake the whole night or otherwise run away to safety. How she wished her father would have warned her in advance about the grass-thatched structures. She was a visitor in the village and had nowhere to escape. On the other hand, her cousin Benita was overly excited. She continued churning out story after story. These stories gradually soothed her anxiety away, and without knowing, she went into deep slumber!

As she woke up the following morning, she thanked God to be alive. What she did not know is that there existed a strong taboo in the village against burning another person's hut. A strange spell or even death was known to befall the arsonist. This was meant to allow everybody to sleep in peace. For that reason, the grass thatched huts thrived. Melisa was nonetheless glad that she had endured an interesting episode that she would live to tell.

The following morning, Melisa's parents woke up to tidying the house and cleaning the compound. Meanwhile, she proceeded to check on her grandparents in the garden. She was amazed at the amount of land they had cultivated since daybreak. Someone ought to have taken a heavy breakfast to exhibit that kind of energy. They had actually taken none! Back in the city, they always had breakfast first thing in the morning. She remembered the many occasions she had her early morning breakfast only to go back to sleep! She suddenly realized how wasteful city dwellers were, eating too much without work.

Her grandmother invited her to try it out on the hoe. As she lifted the soil on the first strike, she was full of excitement. She had a real feeling of farm life. On the fifth attempt, though, she developed fatigue, and her heart beat faster. At that rate, she estimated that she would probably drop down in the next few seconds. However, she had to prove to her grandparents that she was not a weakling. She tried hard to hide her exhaustion. Fortunately, her grandmother, who was quite watchful, stepped in before the embarrassment.

At this point in time, Melisa had become accustomed to surprises. That notwithstanding, one event on that evening would leave her mesmerized. The afternoon heat had subsided when she heard loud voices of jubilant children outside the house. As she came out to inquire, she saw numerous white ants flying around. The children had surrounded the holes from which the insects were emerging. Their parents, who had been alerted by the noise, joined in enthusiastically.

For a moment, Melisa thought that it could be a culture of the community to celebrate such an event, hence the excitement. She was however, taken aback when she saw everybody pick the insects and thrust them right into their mouths. Her clansmen were literally eating live insects! What a marvel! Her grandmother looked at her and noticed the bewilderment. Grandma was quick to reassure her that white ants were, in fact, a traditional delicacy among the Abalukhya tribe. Melisa implored her never to serve the insects as a sole accompaniment for any meal until they went back to the city.

It was the end of day two, and the village was full of adventure. Each passing day would probably bring forth its own puzzles. It was apparent that the city and the village were worlds apart. Melisa could now understand the conduct of students from rural areas while at school. As soon as she landed in high school, she discovered that there was a group of students she could not match. Other than academic lessons, the two groups shared little in common. They rarely ate anything apart from the official school meals. For this reason, they carried neither snacks nor beverages. They cared less that their colleagues had their parents visit them regularly. One particularly carried a toothbrush but never used it, preferring instead to use a wooden stick plucked from the obengele tree! It was now clear that they had been brought up in a different setting. It could be that this holiday experience would help bridge the gap and endear her to comrades from the countryside.